the One Tree

the One Tree

the One Tree

"...All beings have sometimes been
represented by a great tree...

As growth gives rise to fresh buds these
branch out and so by generation I believe it
has been with a great Tree of Life, which fills
the crust of the earth with it's dead and
broken branches, and covers its surface
with its ever branching and
beautiful ramifications."

Charles Darwin, 1859

SeaSquirt
Books

The One Tree

First published in Great Britain in 2006

ISBN 1-905470-18-5 (Paperback)
ISBN 1-905470-19-3 (Hardback)
British Library CIP Data
A catalogue record of this book is available from the British Library

Published by SeaSquirt Books
Ty Ganol   Rhodiad y Brenin   St Davids
Pembrokeshire   Wales   SA62 6PY

Story by David Hughes
Illustration by Richard Perrott
Design by David Hughes and Jane Messore

Printed and bound by Gomer Press Limited
Ceredigion   Wales   SA44 4JL

*This book is dedicated to
the people and City of St Davids in Pembrokeshire, Wales
where it was written.*

Story by
David Pierce Hughes

Illustration by
Richard Perrott

the One Tree

Story by David Pierce Hughes

Illustration by Richard Perrott

Some time ago, before there was anyone to worry about time, most of the land on the planet Earth was covered by trees.

Every so often throughout the ages, before
there was anyone to count time, many of the Earth's
trees were destroyed by sheets of ice from glaciers
or fire from volcanoes. But the trees always fought
back to survive.

After some millions of years, creatures that had
started life in the sea, and then climbed up into the
trees, dropped down from the tree branches.

Some millions of years later, not so very long
ago, these creatures learned to walk on two legs.
And about a million years or so ago (we don't know
exactly), these creatures developed intelligence and
evolved into the people we are today.

This time, a long way from the timeless time, people
developed industry and technology. They became so
powerful that they believed they were the masters of
their destiny, and the destiny of the Earth on which
all trees, and all creatures, and all people depend.

Not far from anywhere
and quite near somewhere,
by a rock near the top of a small hill,
stood a tall, lone tree.

This tree, the One Tree, could see for miles,
across the hills, over the river, down to the
sea. Looking from its highest branch, the
One Tree could not see any other trees.

When the wind blew,
the One Tree sighed and bent,
but always stood bravely,
by the rock on the hill,

not far from anywhere
and quite near somewhere.

One day a boy struggled up the hill and sat down on the rock under the One Tree.

The boy was crying, so the One Tree lowered a long branch and patted him on the shoulder to comfort him.

"Why are you crying?" asked the One Tree.

"Because I feel all alone," said the boy.

"Are you lonely, too?" he asked, for he had noticed the One Tree was all alone.

"No, I am never lonely," said
the One Tree.

"The birds come and nest in my branches.

"The foxes come wandering around my
trunk at night, when the moon is out.

"The winds blow and the rain comes
and quenches my thirst.

"The worms wriggle into their holes
between my roots. Sometimes that tickles.
But I am never alone or sad," said the
One Tree.

Each day after school, the boy would climb up the hill to sit on the rock under the One Tree, and they would talk.

As they talked, the boy began to realise a little more each day that the One Tree always saw the good side of everything.

The One Tree explained:
"I like the wind because it helps seeds to spread to other places and take root, and because it helps the birds to fly long distances to other lands.

"I like the rain, because water helps me to grow taller by feeding my roots.

"And I even like the snow in winter, because it keeps me warm like a blanket when the wind blows cold."

The One Tree explained to the boy that trees breathe out oxygen, which is in the air that people need to survive on Earth. And that trees breathe in carbon dioxide, a gas that people breathe out.

The One Tree said: "I help to keep the air clean on our planet, Earth. And if we look after Earth, then it will look after us."

The One Tree told the boy that it loved:
The change of the seasons,
The rhythm of the rain,
The music of the stream,
The soft touch of the snow,
The music in the wind,
The singing of the birds,
The movement of the clouds.

After several weeks of his talks each day with the One Tree, the boy no longer felt lonely.

Every day after school the boy looked forward to climbing up the hill and sitting on the rock, near the top of the small hill, under the spreading branches of his friend, the One Tree.

Not far from anywhere
and quite near somewhere.

Then one day, the boy's mother told him that the family would be moving to a new town hundreds of miles away in another land.

The boy knew that he would have to go to see his friend, the One Tree, for the last time, for a last chat before he had to move away.

As he climbed the hill he noticed that the soil on the side of the hill, the side he had always climbed, was all churned up.

As he went higher and higher, he saw large tyre tracks and deep ruts wounding the earth.

At last, the boy reached the rock.
All he could see was a large hole in
the ground and a few pieces of roots and
branches scattered around, like broken
arms and legs.

The boy picked up a piece of branch and
held it tight. The stick was all he had to
remind him of his old friend.

They had cut down his friend the One
Tree and dragged it away.

Then the boy sat on the rock and wept.
His tears ran down the rock between his
feet and into the hole where the roots of
the One Tree had been.

The boy sat on the rock for hours.
He kept closing his eyes. He hoped that
when he opened them he would find that
his friend, the One Tree, was still standing
there, brave and tall.

He hoped that the One Tree would pat
him gently on the shoulder with a branch
and comfort him, as he had on that first
day when they became friends.

But there was no touch on his shoulder.
All the boy could hear was the sound of
the wind.

At last, the boy went slowly down the
hill to his home. He had to leave, for
his family were moving away.

29

Many years passed. The boy became a man, tall and strong and brave. He sailed the oceans. He travelled around the world.

He walked over hills and mountains
looking for a place he could call home. And
wherever he went, he never forgot the One
Tree. He always carried the stick that came
from one of One Tree's branches.

More and more years passed and
the man grew older and older. Yet no
matter how far, or where he journeyed,
he never found the right place to settle.

One night the wanderer had a strange
dream. He dreamed he was a boy again. He
dreamed he was in a dark forest where an old
man with green eyes came to him and said:
"You must go to the place where you found
your first friend when you were a boy.
You must go and sit on the rock near the top
of the hill, where you met the One Tree."

So the old man went back to that place, where it all began. He journeyed over oceans. He walked over hills. At last he reached the place where he had found his first friend, the One Tree.

Slowly he climbed the hill, with the help of the stick he always carried. He looked for the terrible ruts in the ground that he remembered from the day they had dragged away his friend, the One Tree.

He was so tired and old. He could hardly raise his feet. He climbed more and more slowly up to the rock at that special place.

Quite near somewhere
and not far from anywhere.

At last he recognised the place, that special place. Some of the ruts in the ground leading to the hole where the One Tree had stood all those years ago were still there.

Not far from anywhere
and quite near somewhere.

The old man sat on the rock, looking at the ground. He began to cry. His tears ran down the rock, just as they had all those years before.

The old man cried and cried. His tears flowed down the rock and into the hole where the One Tree had stood.

Suddenly, a small green leaf pushed its way out of the ground, right before his eyes.

"Thank you," said a voice from the earth between the old man's feet.

"I have been waiting so long for you to come and give me your tears of friendship to feed the roots that were left when my trunk was torn away.

"I knew you would not let me down. I knew that one day you would come and help me to grow back into a tall strong tree."

While he listened to the words from
the earth, the old man had stopped crying.

Now he wept again, this time tears of joy
as he recognised the voice of his old friend,
the One Tree.

As he wept, his tears of friendship
provided more strength to feed the green
shoot that had sprung from the earth at the
special place.

Not far from anywhere
and quite near somewhere.

If you could go there now, if you could
find that special place, near the top of a
small hill, you would have to search hard

to find the rock
where the boy first talked
to his friend, the One Tree.

Now, all around a forest has grown, with
plants and animals and birds and insects
living among many, many trees,

near where the boy
and the One Tree
first met and talked.

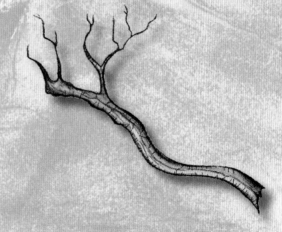

41

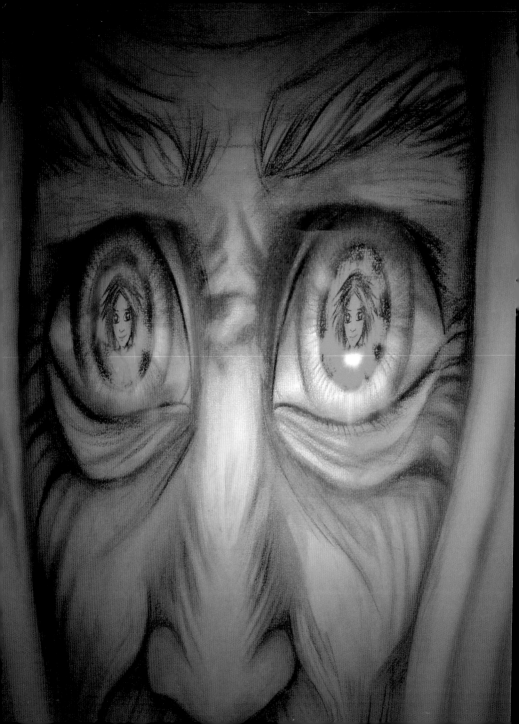

And if you could be in the trees where this forest has grown, you might catch a glimpse of the shape of the shadow of an old man moving in and out of the trees.

And if you could look into the old man's eyes you would see an image of the boy who never stopped believing in his friend the One Tree and the time they shared together.

The timeless time that all the Earth's people share.

Not far from anyone but quite near everyone.

About the paper on which
The One Tree book is printed.

¶ Paper is made from fibres that are found in the cell walls of all plants. The fibres mainly come from plant sources such as wood, bamboo, cotton, jute, or even rice. However wood from trees is the main source of fibres used in paper making. A mixture of water and fibres is filtered through a screen to make a sheet of paper. When the paper is dried chemical bonds form to give the paper its strength.

The One Tree book is printed on paper in which at least 75% of the fibre has been used before. This means it comes from materials that have been recycled.

The main types of papers of which recycled paper is made from are:
- Newspapers, magazines, directories and leaflets.
- Office and computer used paper
- Carboard from boxes and packaging
- Mixed or coloured papers

The remaining fibre comes from 'mill broke'. This means off-cuts and material that was rejected when this part of the fibre was first used at the paper mill. It could be material that has been used before or virgin fibre sourced from managed forests.

NAPM approved
recycled product

Other works by the author, David Hughes:

• Poetry:
Poems One Euro Each
download with Dante

These two books
are published by
www.infestedwaters.co.uk

The author's cottage, near St Davids in Pembrokeshire.

• Childrens' books:
The JimJAZZ mouse series of books
which chart the adventures of
JimJAZZ mouse and his musical friends.
Each book features a different instrument
and explores music and colour.

There are nineteen books in this series which
is published by SeaSquirt Publications. You
can see more at www.jimjazzmouse.com

Further information about conserving trees:
You can see more about the useful conservation
work that the Woodland Trust carries out at
www.woodland-trust.org.uk. David Hughes is
pleased to be a member of the Woodland Trust.